Be Sweet!

Pam Alexander

Text copyright ©2000 by Rhonda Frost Kight
Illustrations copyright ©2000 by Pamela M. Alexander
Printed in the U.S.A.
First U.S. Edition 2001

Library of Congress Cataloging-in-Publication Data
Kight, Rhonda Frost
The Onion Ambassador/Rhonda Frost Kight;
Illustrated by Pamela M. Alexander.
1st U.S. ed.

Summary: South Georgia farmer and wife discover giant onion named Yumion. His
mission is to tell the world about sweet Vidalia onions.
ISBN 0-9709105-0-9
[1. Onion-Fiction. 2. Georgia-Fiction. 3. Vidalia, Georgia-Fiction.
4. Children's poetry, American. 5. Onion-Juvenile poetry.]
I. Alexander, Pamela M., ill. II Title.
Pre-press was performed by Colson Printing Company, Valdosta, GA
Yumion™ used by permission from the Toombs/Montgomery Chamber of Commerce

Printed by Quebecor World/Book Services, Kingport, TN
Published by Be Sweet Publications, Inc.

The Onion Ambassador

Written by: Rhonda Frost Kight

Illustrated by: Pam Alexander

To my family,
my God (The Great Physician),
and to Dr. Vendie H. Hooks III,
who is next on that list.
R.F.K.

To John,
my best supporter,
critic, and friend.
P.M.A.

Special thanks to B.D. and M.L.
For being willing to lend a hand, a foot, or a face
to the project.
We couldn't have asked for better models
in books or in life.

This is the tale of a Vidalia sweet,
not a beautiful girl, but an onion . . . with feet!

On a warm spring day a farmer went out to his onion field to harvest a sprout.

He pulled a few big ones and then cut their stems; shook off the dirt and took them with him.

His wife cooked them up in a specialty dish, and she said to her husband, the farmer, "I wish

Those words were planted like seeds in his head,
and the next day the farmer jumped out of his bed.

With a yank of her hand he took up his bride,
and she said, "Where're we going?" as they hurried outside.

"To the field," he said quickly, "to pull up a few more of those onions to see if they're all mild to the core!"

They chopped and they tasted; not one tear did drop,
"These onions are SWEET, not strong, WHAT A CROP!"

They smiled for they knew they had uncovered a vegetable secret not yet discovered.

"By golly," the farmer said with a grin,
as they yanked on the large stems again and again.

Until finally the onion was standing up tall, wearing gloves, big brown shoes, and blue overalls.

The farmer said "Wow!" his wife yelled out, "Great!
I bet you'll be known all over this state!"

"You're right," said the Yumion, "and I'd better get started!"

He turned with a smile and as he departed, he said a few words he was bound to repeat: